Six Feet Apart

Michelle Wilbern

Katrina Gross

Preface

The idea for this book came to me one day while teaching during the coronavirus pandemic. I realized, when returning to the classroom for the first time in over a year, that there were no books to support students with the transition to in-person school. The school building was foreign to me as the teacher, and I knew my students, despite doing my best to make everything seem normal, would feel out of place. On the first day of in-person school, one student sneezed in my classroom. I could sense the discomfort on this student's face, and I decided that this was a teachable moment. The class broke into a conversation about how, during this time, we need to be kind, and recognize that sneezing is a natural thing that is okay. I went home that night and wrote this manuscript, thinking about the social and emotional impact of students returning to school during such a stressful and strange year. I hope you enjoy this story as much as I do.

Ella woke up and wanted to play.
"Put on your mask," her mother
would say.

She grabbed her two-layer mask in a rush, running so fast she just missed the bus. "Get in the car, we have to be quick. You don't want to be late for your day with Ms. Nick."

Ella was excited and started to beam. She was going to school and it wasn't on screen!

Ella loved school and she missed her friends. *Will they be there?* she thought, *will they attend?*

Mom drove to school. They were in a big hurry and when they arrived, Ella started to worry.

Follow the X's. She read the bold words. Ella kept walking but found it absurd. *Was this all being done to prevent getting sick?* Ella worried and worried and then saw Ms. Nick.

In the classroom the desks were spaced six feet apart and the walls were all covered with health safety art.

My Classroom. My Teacher. Ella started to smile. Her fears were all gone, at least for a while. Evelyn, Ace, and Brianna too, all of her friends were arriving at school.

As Ella unpacked, she felt in her nose a tingling sensation and everyone knows, the tickle you get, the tingle you feel, when a sneeze is coming. Ella thought, *is this for real? What will they think of me? Will they get sick?* She sank in her chair, but the sneeze came on quick.

Ms. Nick sensed the problem and took quick command. She walked over to Ella with tissue in hand. "Don't worry Ella, it's just a little sneeze." "Take this tissue," and she smiled with ease. Ella covered her face, but it was no use. She sneezed into her mask and not the tissue.

She wanted to cry. Her cheeks turned red. She started to sniffle, but then Ms. Nick said, "When things are different, and you feel out of place remember to have kindness and a little bit of grace. We can work together, and help each other through. The pandemic will end, and this strangeness will too."

Ms. Nick handed Ella a clean new mask, Ella smiled because she didn't have to ask. "Let's all gather round, there's work to be done! School is a bit different, but we can still have fun."

Ella soon realized, she started to see that returning to school would be really easy.

"Kindness" Ms. Nick said, "will help us get through." And kindness was just what Ella would do.

About the Author

My name is Michelle Wilbern and I am an educator, Ph.D. student, and mother. I love children's literature and have always enjoyed using stories to support my students' growth both academically and socially and emotionally. This is my first published work and I hope it is not my last.

About the Illustrator

Hi! I'm Katrina. Thank you for taking the time to pick up this book. This is the first book I've ever illustrated, and I hope it is not the last. I hope you enjoy the story as much as I do. I was a student during COVID, just like Ella. I hope you, dear reader, will utilize this book to help your own students. I see myself in Ella and you may see yourself in her too.